ni hao, kai-lan

Meet Kai-lan!

adapted by Mickie Matheis
based on the screenplay "Everybody's Hat Parade" written by Bradley Zweig
illustrated by Jason Fruchter and Aka Chikasawa

Simon Spotlight/Nickelodeon
New York   London   Toronto   Sydney

Based on the TV series *Ni Hao, Kai-lan!*™ as seen on Nick Jr.®

SIMON SPOTLIGHT
An imprint of Simon & Schuster Children's Publishing Division
1230 Avenue of the Americas, New York, New York 10020
For information about special discounts for bulk purchases, please contact Simon & Schuster Special Sales
at 1-866-506-1949 or business@simonandschuster.com.
Manufactured in the United States of America
10
ISBN 978-1-4169-8502-0
1109 LAK

Ni hao! I'm Kai-lan! Look — Mr. Sun is sleeping. Let's tickle him to wake him up. Stretch out your arms, wiggle your fingers, and tickle, tickle, tickle!

Mr. Sun, *ni hao*! Ooh — sun fuzzies! They tickle!

What's that? I hear somebody singing. It's my Grandpa! I call him *YeYe*. Let's go see him.

YeYe is wearing a big hat. He calls it a *mao zi*. *YeYe* made it himself.

YeYe's hat is way too big for me. He's so silly!
I'm going to make my own *mao zi*! Will you help me? Yeah! Come on, let's go, go, go!

This is my friend, Mr. Hoppy. Mr. Hoppy, *ni hao*! Mr. Hoppy, may I please use your lily pad to make my hat?

"Ribbit! Ribbit!" replies Mr. Hoppy.

Xie xie! Thank you!

Now it's time to make my hat. I'll just fold the lily pad here and pinch it there. Ta-da! Do you like my *mao zi*? *Xie xie!* Thank you!

Here's my friend Rintoo. He's a tiger! Rintoo likes my *mao zi*. He thinks it's awesome.

Our friends Tolee the koala and Hoho the monkey like my hat too. I have an idea! Let's all make hats! Then we can have a really big hat parade!

Ready . . . set . . . time to make *mao zi*!

Rintoo and Hoho found twigs, pinecones, and leaves for their hats. Tolee found some feathers. Each hat is going to be very special!

I'd like to add something yellow and pretty to my *mao zi*. Do you see something yellow?
You're right! A yellow flower! Now my hat is really special! *Xie xie!* Thank you!

Hao xiang. Something smells yummy! What could it be?
It's Mr. Fluffy's bakery! Mr. Fluffy makes yummy cakes.
    Mr. Fluffy says he'll make a **special** cake for our hat parade.
Xie xie, Mr. Fluffy! Thank you!

Oh, no! My hat! The wind is blowing it away! Let's call our friend Lulu the rhino to help us get it. Say "Lulu! Lulu!"

Super! Lulu's flying over.
Lulu, *ni hao*! We need your help. My hat is on the roof.

She got it! *Xie xie,* Lulu! Thank you!
Lulu says, *"Bu ke qi.* You're welcome!"
Lulu says she will make a *mao zi* for the parade too. Yeah!

Rintoo and Hoho love their hats!
Rintoo used twigs, leaves, and pinecones to make his *mao zi*.
So did Hoho.

Uh-oh! Rintoo looks mad. "Hoho! You copied me!" he says.
Rintoo wants Hoho to take off his hat. Hoho shakes his head no. Now Rintoo stomps away and says he doesn't want to be in our parade anymore!

We gotta, gotta try to find the reason why Rintoo stomped away.

Do you think Rintoo is mad that Hoho copied his hat? I think so too.

What can we try? It's up to me and you.
Rintoo's mad that Hoho copied his hat. We'll figure out what to do!

I know! Let's ask Mr. Fluffy what he does when someone copies one of his special cakes.

Look! Mr. Fluffy has finished making the special cake for our parade. And here comes his assistant, Mei Mei the polar bear, with a cake that looks exactly the same.

"Mr. Fluffy is going to be mad that you copied his cake, Mei Mei," says Rintoo.

"Actually," says Mr. Fluffy, "I'm happy. Sometimes it's okay to be copied. It makes me feel so good that Mei Mei liked my cake so much that she copied it!"

"Maybe Hoho copied my hat because he liked it so much!" says Rintoo. "And that makes my hat even more special!"

Rintoo says he's glad that Hoho's *mao zi* is just like his. Rintoo starts to sing.

"I got it! I got it! It's really really true! I got it! I got it! I know just what to do!"

"When you make something, and your friend copies you, sometimes it means that they really like it too! And that makes it even more special!"

But wait! Hoho's hat is not exactly like Rintoo's. What's missing?

Right — a pinecone! Now Rintoo's hat and Hoho's hat are exactly the same!

Hooray! It's time for the parade! You're a really good friend. You helped Rintoo, and you helped me make the best hat parade ever! You make my heart feel super happy!

Zai jian! Good-bye!